Ariana Rose:
A Story of Courage

By Ariana Feiner

First Edition, 2014

ISBN: 978-0-9906826-0-8

Ariana Feiner Publishing

www.arianafeiner.com

*To all children, especially those who have delicate medical conditions —
always keep hope and remember to smile.*

This is a girl named Ariana Rose.
She likes to draw pictures and wear dress up clothes.

She loves going to school to see her best friend,
Dancing, and singing, and playing pretend.

Ariana has green eyes, pink cheeks, and gold curls,
But something makes her different from the other boys and girls.

She plays tag at recess and runs all around,
But then she gets tired and has to sit down.

4

Ariana feels dizzy when she gets home that night.
She tells her mom that she doesn't feel right.

She feels kind of funny and feels kind of sore —
A kind of weak feeling she'd never felt before.

Mom calls the doctor to ask what to do.
The doctor says, "Come here tomorrow at two."

7

So mom takes Ariana to Dr. Levine,
Where they wait in a room that's chilly and clean.

The doctor pops out and calls her name.
Ariana goes with him still feeling the same.

He examines her ears,
her throat, and her eyes.

He listens to her heart
and measures her size.

Ariana's doctor tells her after they're through,
"You have a long term illness, and I can help you.

Follow this schedule of medicine and rest,
Have a positive attitude, and do your best.

It will get easier after a while,
So you must keep hope, and remember to smile."

Ariana takes her medicine as the doctor requests.
She comes back home, has a snack, and she rests.

The very next week Ariana feels better.
She goes back to school in her favorite pink sweater.

Her friends are happy to see her and ask,
"Are you okay? We missed you in class."

Ariana describes what she has to her peers.
They gather around her with open ears.

"I take special medicine and get extra rest,
Have a positive attitude, and do my best.

It will get easier after a while,
So I always keep hope and remember to smile."

Ariana tells her friends not to worry or fret.
She is still the same girl she was when they met.

She's brave and she's strong from her head to her toes.
This is a girl named Ariana Rose.

The End

Special Thanks

Special thanks to my Galloway School community whose encouragement and friendship always lifts me up. To Daniel Yellin for his bright ideas and analytical mind. To Janet Roberts for her kindness, creativity, and wisdom. And especially to my wonderful family Lisa, Cliff, and Isaac for all their love.